W9-BWW-003

HENRY'S
FOURTH OF JULY

by Holly Keller

Greenwillow Books
New York

Library of Congress Cataloging in Publication Data
Keller, Holly.   Henry's Fourth of July.
Summary: Henry has a fun-filled day celebrating
the Fourth of July with his family and friends.
1. Children's stories, American.
[1. Fourth of July—Fiction.
2. Picknicking—Fiction] I. Title.
PZ7.K28132He 1985   [E]   84-13707
ISBN 0-688-04012-8
ISBN 0-688-04013-6 (lib. bdg.)

FOR SUSAN AND AVA
WITH LOVE

Henry opened his eyes
and looked out the window.
The sky was blue and
the sun was hot.
Just right for the Fourth of July.

This year he could stay up to see the fireworks.
Mama had promised.

Mama got baby Jake ready for the picnic.

Papa packed the big basket.
"Don't forget the pickles," Mama said.

Cousin Gertie made a paper flag for Henry to carry.
Mama put Jake in the stroller. Then they were ready to go.

Uncle Joe brought the watermelons.

Mrs. Murphy brought a wagonful of corn.

They got there just in time for the parade.

Papa brought potato sacks for races.
Henry climbed into one and Mama
tied it around his middle.

"Get ready, get set, go!"
Uncle Joe bellowed. Henry bounced across
the finish line in third place.

Mrs. Murphy gave out the prizes.
Henry won a little bear.

"A swim in the pond will
cool us off," Mama said.

Henry couldn't swim all the way to the raft.

"But you are very good at floating," Papa said.

After the picnic Uncle Joe dressed up as a clown.

A photographer took funny pictures.

And a dixieland band played music for a dance contest.
Papa tried hard to win.

"Will the fireworks be soon?" Henry asked.
"Very soon," Papa said.

"Come on," Mama said at last. "Let's go up
on the hill. We can see better from there."

Henry waited. He thought it would never start.

All at once the sky was bright with color.

Henry counted
12 different designs.

When it was over, Papa carried Henry home.

"It went too fast," Henry said.

Mama smiled. "It always does," she said.

"Can we go again next year?"

"Of course," said Mama.

Henry pulled his little bear under
the covers and went to sleep.